Level: 5.8
Points: 1

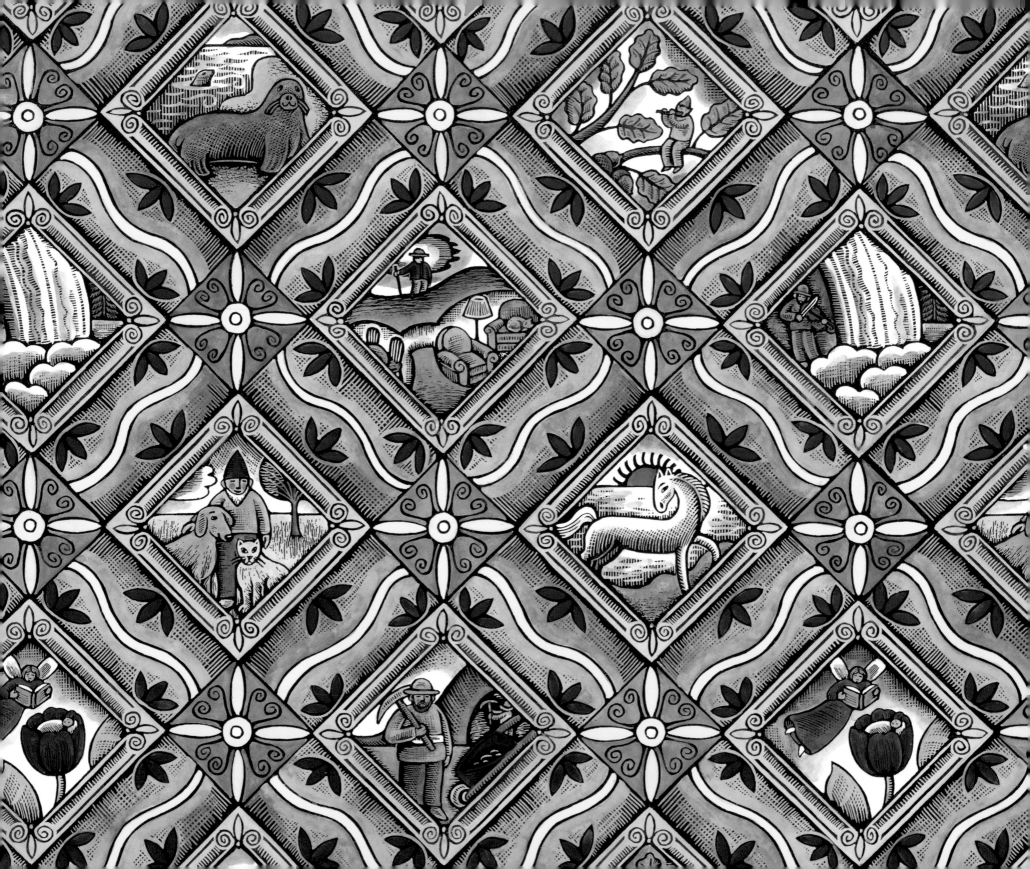

The Hidden Folk

To the trooping fairies:
Emily, Marit, Kaitlin, Caroline, Kelsey, Margo, and Liz.
May your sense of wonder never desert you.
—L. L.-L.

To my sisters,
Cindy, Amy, Laurie, and Stephanie, with love.
—B. K.

Text copyright © 2004 by Lise Lunge-Larsen
Illustrations copyright © 2004 by Beth Krommes

www.houghtonmifflinbooks.com

The text of this book is set in Berkeley Oldstyle.
The illustrations are scratchboard.

Library of Congress Cataloging-in-Publication Data is on file.
ISBN 0-618-17495-8

Manufactured in China
SCP 10 9 8 7 6 5 4 3 2 1

The Hidden Folk

Stories of Fairies, Dwarves, Selkies, and Other Secret Beings

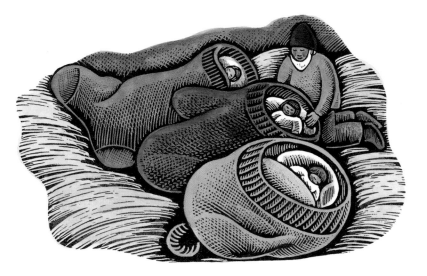

by **Lise Lunge-Larsen**   illustrated by **Beth Krommes**

Houghton Mifflin Company

Boston 2004

Contents

An Introduction

For as long as there have been people, there have been stories about beings whose presence we feel but whom we cannot see, at least not ordinarily. Do they really exist? The many legends full of references to the fairy folk or leprechauns and to such places as fairy mounds or enchanted forests certainly support the idea of their existence. Indeed, until modern times, with our tendency to believe only what the eye can behold (sometimes with the help of telescopes and microscopes), the presence of the hidden folk was widely accepted throughout the world.

So who are they? Where did they come from? And where do they live? At least one story tells us:

When God expelled Adam and Eve from the Garden of Eden, they settled down in the land to the east. They had a great many children, and Eve was frequently overwhelmed with all the work of looking after so many little ones.

One morning, the Lord God surprised Adam and Eve with a visit. Eve was terribly embarrassed because she was not yet a very good housekeeper. She was even more ashamed when God asked to see her children, for she had had time to clean up only two of them. The rest looked like a little band of ragamuffins, all unkempt and hair sticking out.

Flustered, Eve hid away all the untidy little children and brought out only the two that she had cleaned and dressed.

"Here are my children, God," she said.

But, of course, God sees and knows everything, and He knew what Eve had done. Looking at her sternly, He said, "Those children who are seen shall continue to be seen, but those who are hidden shall forever remain hidden from sight."

And so it was.

We are the descendants of Eve's two clean and tidy children. Those who were hidden became the ancestors of all the hidden folk. They are really our siblings, our hidden selves.

The hidden folk are as varied in character as we are. Some are kind and gentle; some are quick to anger and resentment. Some live very close to humans; others live farther away. They are all around, but are usually invisible. Their time is the in-between time: the space between the seasons, like Halloween or early spring; the daily transition periods of dusk and dawn; and especially Midsummer Night's Eve and the winter solstice. On these days time stands still for a little while as the length of the day begins to reverse itself. This is when a crack appears in the surface of the earth that allows these beings to make themselves known to us.

The hidden folk are also more likely to show themselves when we encounter periods of being "in-between," when we stand on the threshold between experiences. The events can be as serious as being gravely ill, hovering between life and death; or as joyful as being pregnant, not without child but not yet a mother, either. All of adolescence is such a period: neither childhood nor adulthood. To some very rare humans, the hidden folk are always visible. These humans are called second sighted and are usually born on a Sunday. It is also possible to gain second sight by rubbing an ointment of four-leaf clovers on your eyelids.

The following stories will tell you about some, not all, of the hidden folk, about where they live and how you can find evidence of them even today. I wanted to give readers a glimpse into the world of the hidden folk in the way I caught glimpses of them growing up in Norway. I knew where the wood elves played their music and which hills were inhabited by hill folk. My grandmother met a river horse, and I know we had a nisse in our attic.

The hidden folk inhabit every country in the world, but like beloved children they have many different names: The river sprite is called *stromkarl* in Sweden, *hantu ban dan* in Malaysia, and *vilcanota* in Peru. Dwarves are known in Spain as *duendes*, in Slavic countries as *karliki*, in Mexico as *chanques,* and in Zaire they are called *biloko*. The stories in this collection are all from the northern regions of Europe. I found that I could tell only the stories of the hidden folk whom I personally know—the folk I know the way I know and love my old friends.

The hidden folk are truly everywhere. If you know how and when to look, you'll spot them even in your neighborhood. And then, if you name them yourself, they'll always belong to you.

The Stories

Flower Fairies

Of all the hidden folk, fairies are perhaps the best known. There are many kinds of fairies, from trooping fairies, who live in big groups, to solitary fairies, who like to live alone. Perhaps the best-loved fairies are the flower fairies, for they are the caretakers of all flowers. They are about the size of a small dragonfly, have gossamer wings, and fly as fast as hummingbirds. They usually live wherever there are flowers, especially in forest meadows.

Flower fairies love flowers so much that some of them find their way into our gardens. In fact, the more flowers you plant, the more likely it is that the fairies will find you, especially if you plant flowers they can sit or sleep in. Their favorite is the tulip because in the spring, when their babies are born, they can lay them down inside the petals and rock them to sleep.

Flower fairies are usually friendly, but if you offend them or mistreat their flowers, they can create quite a bit of mischief, often with interesting results.

The Ivory Cups

Before sunup one spring morning, a troop of fairies went to gather morning dew. Carrying their tiny ivory cups, they flitted among the trees, played hide-and-seek in the ferns and grasses, and danced on the pale moonbeams. As they came near a meadow, loud hissing and roaring broke the quiet of the early dawn. Quickly, the fairies ducked under some leaves. They hung their cups on blades of grass and quietly crept forward to see what was happening.

As they peeked out from under the ferns and grasses, a terrible sight met their eyes. In the middle of the meadow, a young knight was fighting a dragon all by himself. The dragon was an enormous beast with great webbed wings that fanned the flames of fire spouting from his mouth. He had a long tail with spikes at the tip, which he lashed around.

The young knight was badly wounded. Blood streamed through his armor, his face and hands were scorched, and he was so exhausted that he fell to his knees. As the fairies watched in horror, the dragon reared up for his final attack. It flew high up into the air, lashed its tail, and blew fiery hot flames at the knight as it plunged toward him. With the last of his strength, the knight staggered to his feet. He lifted his sword with both hands, and when the dragon was nearly upon him, he thrust his sword upward with all his might. The sword penetrated deep into the dragon's chest and pierced his heart. With a roar that shook the trees, the dragon fell down dead.

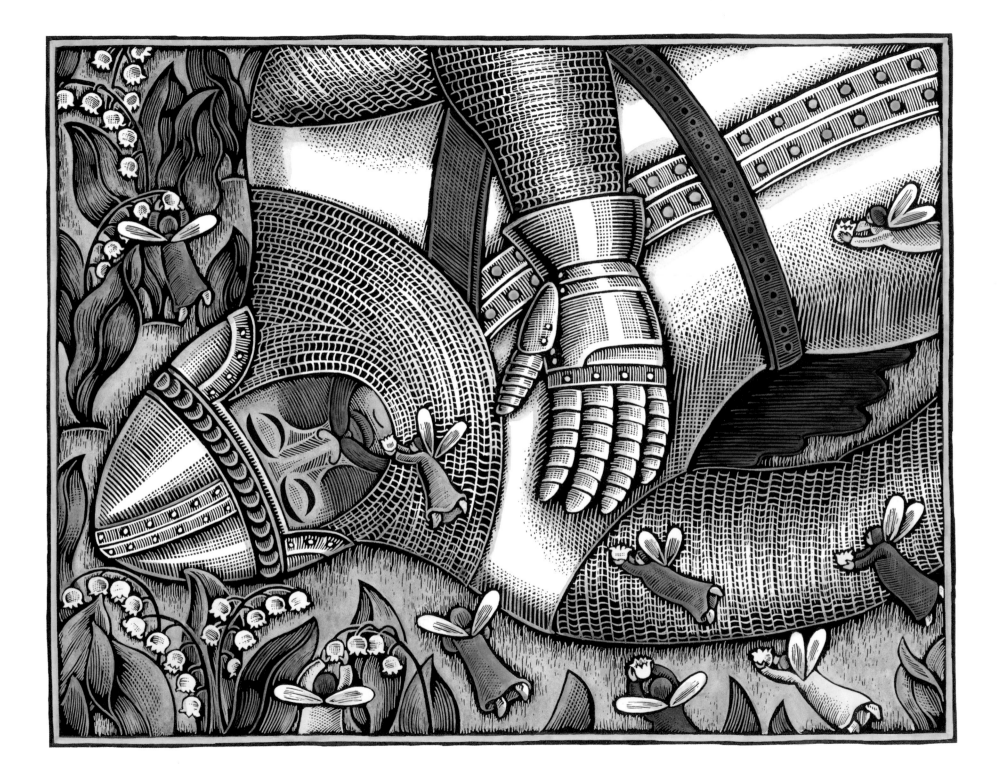

But the knight fell too. Cut by the dragon's claws and burned by its fiery breath, he lay unconscious on the ground.

Cautiously, the fairies crept from their hiding places and flew to the knight's side. His breath was raspy and uneven. Unless the fairies did something, his wounds would kill him. Quickly, they seized their little ivory cups and flitted off through the woods.

Faster than light they flew until, deep in the forest, they came to a small spring. From here flowed the water of life. The fairies dipped their little cups into the spring and flew off again to the meadow where the knight lay dying. One by one, each fairy carefully poured a single drop of the water of life onto his lips. Then they hung their cups on blades of grass and settled around him to watch.

Slowly, the knight licked his lips and swallowed the precious drops. Soon he began to breathe more evenly. The fairies clapped their tiny hands in excitement. They had saved him!

But as the knight stirred, noises came from the forest. It was the village people coming to see how their champion had fared in the battle with the dragon. In great haste, the fairies flew away, forgetting their little cups on the blades of grass.

A little later, when the sun rose and shone on the cups, a wonderful thing happened. The ivory cups became permanently attached to the blades of grass. They became the flowers we know today as lilies of the valley. Every spring you can see them at the edge of the forest, where they grow in memory of how the little fairies saved the young knight. The wonderful scent from the water of life is so strong that it lingers on, even today.

Why couldn't these fairies just come back for their cups? Because if the sun shines on fairies, they immediately turn to dust—fairy dust.

Tulips and Parsley

A long time ago there lived an old woman who had an especially beautiful and large bed of tulips. The fairies loved these flowers. Each spring evening, just when the last rays of the sun dipped below the horizon, they gently placed their tiny babies inside the tulips and rocked them to sleep. In return, the fairies made the tulips bloom as long and smell as wonderful as roses.

When the old woman died, a gentleman who didn't care for flowers at all bought her house. He dug up the tulip bed and planted row upon row of herbs instead.

That spring, when the fairies arrived with their newborns, there was not a single tulip in sight. They searched the entire garden but found only broad-leaved herbs. Furious, the fairies placed their babies under some ferns and attacked the herbs. They ripped up the edges of the leaves with their little fingers and spat at them with all their might. Then they picked up their babies and flew off in a huff.

The next morning, when the gentleman came outside, his sweet-smelling herbs were gone. Looking down on his garden, he saw only row upon row of a funny-looking plant. Its edges were ragged and crinkled, and when he tasted it, he nearly choked because it was so bitter. That plant was the herb we now know as parsley. The ragged edges of the leaves are from the fairies' tiny fingers ripping them up, and the bitter taste is from fairy spit!

Usually fairies are dressed in the colors of the flowers they protect.

Gnomes

Of all the hidden folk, gnomes probably like humans the most and live the closest to us. There is a certain kind of gnome called a "nisse" who lives on a farm. Nisses are usually friendly and take good care of the farm animals. Today, with so few farms left, the number of nisses has declined, and they have become much more shy of humans. Still, some have moved into towns, especially to houses with animals. Do you have a dog or a cat that is especially content and whose fur is sleek and shiny? Then you may have a nisse helping out with your pets.

You can recognize a nisse by his size: He is even smaller than a one-year-old child, but he lives to be hundreds of years old. Like all gnomes, he wears a red pointed cap. Do you lose a lot of socks, hats, and mittens? It is the nisse who takes them: he uses them as sleeping bags and blankets for his children.

Nisses bring good luck to anyone who treats them kindly. But if you are mean to your nisse or make fun of him, watch out! Despite his tiny size, he is incredibly strong, and anyone who teases him will get into trouble, just like the boy in this story.

The Nisse's Revenge

Once there lived a nisse who loved to dance. As soon as he had given food and water to the animals and brushed all the horses, he would climb up into the hayloft and practice his jumps and leaps. He was an excellent dancer, and at competitions he could swing the nisse women faster and leap higher than any of the other nisses.

One day when he was practicing in the loft above the cow stalls, he leapt so high and landed with such force that—*crack!*—the board in the loft floor split and his little leg broke straight through.

Jack, one of the farm lads, was in the stalls when he saw the little leg dangling through the hole in the ceiling.

Well, well! If it isn't the nisse, thought Jack. *Now I'll have some fun!* Before the nisse could pull his leg out, Jack grabbed a pitchfork and poked him in the leg.

"Ouch!" screamed the nisse and wrenched his leg out of the hole as fast as he could.

"That'll teach you to dance in the hayloft!" Jack hollered. Then he laughed and laughed at how he had surprised the nisse.

At dinner, Jack was still chuckling to himself, and the farmer wanted to know what was so funny.

"Well, I took a good crack at our nisse today," said Jack, laughing. "That fellow was dancing so hard, his leg broke through a floorboard in the hayloft. I gave him quite a jab with the pitchfork!"

"You didn't give me just one jab," shouted the nisse from outside the window. "You gave me three, because there were three prongs on that pitchfork. But I'll pay you back—just you wait and see!"

Jack only shrugged his shoulders and continued his dinner. He wasn't the least bit afraid, for what could such a tiny little fellow do to him? Jack was a tall and strong fifteen-year-old boy and figured he could handle anything. But the farmer shook his head knowingly.

That night, as Jack lay in his bed sleeping, the nisse sneaked into the house, up the stairs, and into Jack's room. Swiftly and silently, the nisse grabbed him and ran outside. There he gripped Jack by the legs, swung him around a few times, and flung him right over the house! Then he ran around to the other side so fast that he was able to catch Jack before he hit the ground. Again, the nisse swung Jack around, tossed him over the house, and ran around to catch him.

Jack, a very sound sleeper, was now as wide awake as he had ever been. He screamed in fright, "Please stop! I'm sorry I poked you. I'll do anything you want and I'll never bother you again, I promise."

But that nisse was mad! He kept up his game till he had tossed Jack over the house eight times. The ninth time he finally did as the boy had begged. He stopped, letting him fall—right into a great mud puddle, where he landed with a giant splash.

Then the nisse burst into such loud peals of laughter that everyone on the farm woke up. The farmer and his wife, children, and servants all came running out in their nightshirts to see what was the matter. When they saw Jack, the farm hand, sitting in the puddle all covered with mud, they too burst out laughing.

Poor Jack! He learned his lesson the hard way, but learn it he did. From then on, he worked hard and was kind to everyone, especially to the nisse.

The Hill Folk

L ike the nisses, the hill folk also live close to humans, but they dwell underground, in hillsides or inside mounds. Their houses are warm and snug and very clean even though they are made of earth. One of their greatest fears is that humans will build their houses on top of their underground homes. Then all the spills and leaks and noises from the human house above will travel down into the hill-folk house below and make life miserable for them.

The hill folk look very much like us, only they are much much smaller and have pale, almost gray skin because they never see daylight. They may come out at dusk or at dawn, but you won't see them unless *they* want you to.

The hill folk are as fond of their homes as we are of ours, and, as you will see in this story, they will do almost anything to protect them.

The Battle for Bornholm

Once upon a time, Denmark was at war with England, and the English fleet, led by the famous admiral Lord Nelson, anchored off the Danish island of Bornholm. Inside nearly every hill and mound along the coast of Bornholm dwelled a great many hill folk. For hundreds of years, their snug underground homes had been quiet and undisturbed, for the Danes knew how to live in harmony with their hidden neighbors. No Dane would do anything so rude as to build a house on top of a hill-folk dwelling.

The hill folk of Bornholm were terribly worried about a possible invasion. If the English took over, would they be as courteous as the Danes? Or would they tear up the hillsides to build their own homes with no regard for the dwellers in the ground below? Of course, the Danes too were worried about their own homes, and posted an army to protect the island. Every day and night hundreds of soldiers stood guard, watching to see if the English would start firing and sending in troops. But no attack came. The fleet remained anchored, doing nothing.

After weeks of this, the Danish soldiers grew bored and restless. Gradually they relaxed their guard. At night fewer and fewer soldiers stayed up.

One dark fall night a young, low-ranked soldier named Soren was alone on the watch. All the others had left for a festival in town. And this was just what the English were waiting for. Under cover of darkness, they quietly lifted their anchors and sailed toward shore. Soren neither heard nor saw a thing, until all at once *BOOM* went a cannon and fire erupted around him.

Poor Soren! He screamed with fright and didn't know what to do. Should he try to shoot and protect the shore all by himself? Or should he abandon his post and run into town? Frantic, he dashed back and forth, calling for help, while the English launched boat after boat full of soldiers to capture the land.

With the English practically on the beach, Soren turned around, ready to run away from his post, when he heard small voices shouting to him, "Fire, fire!"

He looked around but could see nobody. Again he heard, "Fire! Fire!" Then something cool ran over his eyelids, and when he looked again, he saw an entire

To tell if a hill is a suitable place for your house, place a rock in each corner where you plan to build. Leave the rocks a week or so. If they have been moved, the hill is inhabited by the hill folk.

army of tiny people approaching. They came galloping on little ponies, piping and drumming and rattling their sabers and guns. Now Soren realized that the hill folk had blown on his eyelids so he could see that they had come to help.

He hurried to fire a shot, for he knew that the hill folk could never shoot first in a battle among humans. No sooner had he fired than the hill folk grabbed their tiny guns and began to shoot.

PAF, PAF, PAF went their guns, and out blew tiny shots. They aimed with amazing accuracy. Every shot hit its mark. Off flew the hats of the English. Loud shouts and yelps of pain could be heard, for each of the bullets hit like a bee sting. The hill folk fired volley after accurate volley. For the English, it was like being attacked by an angry swarm of bees. They tried to fire back, but they could not see their enemy, so not a single bullet hit its mark.

More and more hill folk came riding out of the mounds, shooting their muskets and arrows. Some rode right down to the shore, poking the enemy with their swords and sabers.

Finally, it became too much for the English. They were covered with welts, which stung and burned. The tiny bullets ripped their clothes and hats, and the saber wounds gave them crippling backaches.

As fast as they could, the English sailed away from Bornholm and never attacked again. Although Lord Nelson was a mighty admiral who beat even Napoleon's fleet, that day he was no match for the hill folk protecting their homes.

The hill folk can see in the dark and usually travel at night. If they need to go out in daylight, they can take on the shape of small animals such as toads or mice. If you see an unusual toad or mouse, be courteous. It may be a hill person, and your politeness is sure to be rewarded.

Elves

Elves live in and among oak trees. There they play in the branches, dance on the grass, or rest in the leaves. They can seem very much like fairies, but they are a little larger and do not have wings. They love to sing and their voices are as sweet as warm, soft air.

Elves, like nisses, are extremely fond of dancing. Often they gather in meadows, where they form rings. If you should walk along a meadow one morning and see stripes or circles in the dewy grass, you will know that the elves were there dancing in the night.

Elves can be divided into two types, light elves and dark elves. The main difference is that dark elves are taller and very dangerous to humans. You must take care never to eat or drink anything offered to you by a dark elf. It will cause you to lose all your sense, and you'll never be yourself again. The best way to tell dark elves from light elves is to see them from behind; dark elves have hollow backs!

The Wedding Feast

Should you find a flat, smooth, round stone in a meadow, leave it there. It is an Elf-Mill, a special stone the elves rest on.

Once upon a time, the elves of Saxony decided to hold a wedding feast in a beautiful castle that belonged to the count of Saxony. At midnight on the night of the wedding, the little elves arrived by the hundreds, jumping in through the keyhole and the cracks in the window. As they landed on the smooth stone floor of the castle, they sounded like peas dropping into a pot.

The noise woke up the old count, who was sleeping in the hall in his high four-poster bed. When he peeked through the bed curtains to see what was making the noise, he was amazed at the sight of so many little people. They were all dressed in white and emitted a wonderful brightness that lit up the room as if by moonbeams.

When they realized the count had seen them, the elves were dismayed. But one of their heralds approached the old man and addressed him with the utmost courtesy.

"Since we have come uninvited to your home and disturbed your sleep, would you do us the honor of sharing in our festivities?" he asked.

"I will join your company," answered the count in a friendly tone, "since my sleep has already been interrupted."

"We have, however, one request to make," added the herald.

"Yes?" asked the count.

Nodding toward the old countess, who lay fast asleep in the bed, the herald said, "It is that you alone shall be present and that none of your people shall look on with you."

"I shall wake or call no one," said the old count, and he slipped out of bed in his nightshirt and nightcap. He carefully drew the curtains shut around the four-poster bed and the sleeping countess and tiptoed over to the assembled elves. A small elf woman was introduced to him for his dancing partner.

Now all was made ready. Little torchbearers took their places, and the cricket musicians struck up a tune. Soon the elves were dancing merrily around. The count did his best, but he found it difficult to keep up with the little woman. She jumped away so lightly that he kept losing her in the dance, and she could twirl in the air with such speed that he ran out of breath trying to keep up.

Suddenly, in the middle of a dance, the music ceased. All the elves vanished into slits in the doors, or mouse holes, or anywhere there was a corner to slip into.

Confused, the count looked around, and then he saw that the door had been opened and a beautiful, tall elf maiden stood in the doorway. She wore a gold crown on her head, and her dress blazed and sparkled with precious stones. She waved her hand, and through the door floated a large number of elves. It was as though a gust of cold damp air entered with these elves, and, indeed, they seemed to be clad in some kind of mist.

The old count shivered a little, but then the maiden with the crown approached him. She held a golden cup in her hand and offered it to the count.

"I see my cousins have quite worn you out and not even offered you their food and wine," she said with a sweet smile. "Have a drink of this and dance with me instead."

Now the count was not a fool. He knew better than to taste of elf drink, but he took the cup from the elf maiden and, pretending to want a drink, lifted it to his lips.

Some elves are called wood elves. They live inside oak trees and can interchange form with them. At midnight you can see these trees walking around.

Then quickly he tossed the liquid over his shoulder. It landed on the bed curtain and burned a great big hole in it. A few drops fell on the countess's cheek and burned her skin! With a cry of pain she woke up.

Shrieking in fury, the elf queen leaped at the count and tried to grab her golden cup, but he merely stepped aside.

"Give me my cup," she hissed. Just then the herald stepped out of a dark corner and shouted, "Throw the cup here." The count did, and with a triumphant cry, the herald grabbed it and escaped through the window.

Immediately, the elf maiden and her people gave chase, and when they turned around, the old count clearly saw that their backs were as hollow as bread troughs. It was the queen of the dark elves herself who had come to destroy the wedding and punish the old count for allowing the light elves to celebrate in his home.

The light elves, though, were grateful to the old count. He never saw them again, but they made sure that he and his family enjoyed good health and good fortune ever after. It was their way of thanking the count and making amends to the countess for the two small burn marks, which she carried on her cheek for the rest of her life.

Dwarves

Dwarves are often confused with gnomes, but they are much bigger, with very stocky and sturdy bodies. Their faces are broad and handsome, and the men often wear beards. They live deep inside the mountains, where they mine and work their metals. Nowadays dwarves are rarely seen, but in the old days they had much exchange with humans. It is from them that we first learned how to find metal and fashion it into weapons, tools, and jewelry. In fact, there are hundreds of reports of people bringing their broken tools to dwarves to be mended.

Dwarves have a tremendous appetite and are known to steal food wherever it is left out. Mostly, though, dwarves are kind and always disposed to help someone in need, as you'll see in this story.

The Silver King

To have your tool
fixed, leave it behind a
dwarf rock—a large
solitary boulder at the foot
of a mountain.
This is the entry to a
dwarf dwelling.
About a week later, your
tool will be returned,
and it will work better
than ever.

There was once a farmer named Matthew who owed so much money that it looked as if he must sell his farm. Nobody in his village would lend him money, so he went all the way to the capital city to see if there was any way to rescue his property. But there was no help to be had.

Filled with sorrow, he started for home. He had only half a loaf of bread in his pack, yet he felt as though he carried a heavy load. What would become of him and his wife and children? Would they have to sell the farm? Would they survive by begging? Would his children starve?

He walked on till he came to some large boulders. Here he sat down to rest. While Matthew sat sorrowing with his head hung low, a stocky little man arrived and sat down next to him. He looked to be very old, for his face was full of wrinkles, but his eyes were kind. They fell to talking, and the old man was so pleasant that Matthew wanted to share what little he had with him.

He pulled out the half loaf of bread and took a small amount for himself. Then he offered some to the little man. Thanking him for the offer, the man took the bread and ate *all* of it!

Matthew thought that perhaps the man was even hungrier than he was, so he didn't say anything. He just talked some more, and in the end he told the man his entire sad tale.

By this time, it had grown late in the afternoon.

"It's a long way to your village," said the little man. "Why don't you come home with me instead, and I'll give you a place to stay."

Matthew accepted gratefully. He was exhausted and worried about how to tell his wife the bad news. A good night's sleep just might help, he thought.

They set off straight into the spruce forest, the little man leading the way. As soon as they entered the forest it became so dark that Matthew couldn't see a foot ahead.

He stumbled several times, and the little man had to hold him by the arm so he wouldn't get lost. The ground felt strange under his feet too, but he couldn't make out why. After a while it sounded as if they were crossing a bridge, and when they reached the other side it grew lighter. Ahead stood a beautiful farm with many small farms surrounding it. It looked almost like a little town, all bathed in a soft, silvery glow.

"This is my home," said the little man, gesturing to the largest farm.

"You must be very rich," said Matthew, amazed.

"You should know I am king here," the old man replied, and clicked his heels together. For the first time Matthew noticed that the heels of the little man's boots sparkled of pure silver, that he wore a silver belt around his waist and carried a silver staff in his hand. Why, this was a dwarf king!

As he led Matthew into his house, the dwarf king called out to his wife.

"I have invited this farmer home with me. He shared so generously of his bread," he said, winking at Matthew. "I hope we have something for him too."

In no time, handsome servants dressed in fine livery served a splendid meal.

Matthew almost forgot to eat and drink, so busy was he admiring everything. The walls were made of gold and silver and sparkled so that his eyes almost hurt. The table was made of silver and the chairs of gold, with red velvet cushions edged with pearls. Even the dishes and the utensils were made of gold, silver, and copper and with designs so finely wrought that Matthew knew there was nothing like it on Earth.

After the meal, the dwarf king showed Matthew his treasures. There were trunks filled to the brim with gold, silver, and gemstones. There were wall hangings woven

with gold and silver thread depicting scenes from the history of the dwarves. There were more riches here than Matthew had thought existed in the entire world.

Then the dwarf king took him to the workshops, where hundreds of dwarves were hammering and twisting and turning metal into intricate shapes.

Last he led Matthew through a doorway that opened into the mountain behind the farm. They walked deep inside along a passage lit by torches. After a sharp turn, the passage opened up into a huge chamber where an enormous tree grew. The tree was so tall, Matthew couldn't see the top. Its leaves hung down like silver drops and

tinkled slightly in the light breeze from the passage. The trunk was so thick that at least eight people could hold hands around it, and it too sparkled and glimmered in the torchlight.

"This tree is the source of all the silver in the world," said the dwarf king. "Its roots spread around the world, and I and my people are its guardians. My older brother guards the tree of gold and my younger brother the tree of copper," he added.

Then he pulled a pouch out of his pocket and grabbed several handfuls of silver leaves off the tree. Now Matthew saw that the leaves were really silver coins! The dwarf king stuffed the coins into the pouch and handed it to Matthew. "Take this and pay off your debt," he said.

That night, Matthew slept better than he had in years. The next morning the dwarf king guided him back to the boulders and bade him farewell. "Please come back and visit," he said. Matthew was about to thank him for his hospitality, but the little dwarf king had vanished. All that was left was a silvery glint in the air.

Matthew returned home with a light heart. With the silver, he was able to pay off all of his debt, and he prospered to the end of his days, for the pouch of silver never ran out of coins. And though he never met the silver king again, whenever he passed the boulders where he had met him, he thought he saw a glint of silver in the forest.

Dwarves can move invisibly in our world because they wear a small brown invisibility cap. They usually come to taste our food, which they love.

Water Horses

There is a certain kind of hidden creature who lives in deep, quiet lakes. He likes to live alone, so there is only one water horse in each lake. Nobody has ever seen him up close in his true shape, but from a distance he could almost be mistaken for a log—except that his hair is long and silvery. He comes up on land only at dusk or dawn, and then he takes the shape of a beautiful white horse. That's why he's called the water horse. But he is not a real horse, for his hooves point backward. You probably won't notice this, however, because he is so lovely that you will want to stroke and ride him. He may even lie down to entice you onto his back. Be careful! If you climb up, he will take off and plunge into the lake with you. Then your only hope is to call out his name.

The Long Horse

There were once seven children whose names were Nicholas, Molly, Christopher, Charlotte, Netty, Caroline, and Marta. They were done with their chores for the day and now they hurried off to play. For a long time they played by the lake. They sailed bark boats, floated sticks, and skipped rocks. Then they went into the forest to play hide-and-go-seek and capture the flag.

They were so involved in their games that they completely forgot about time. All at once they noticed that it had begun to grow dark. Soon the sun would set. Quickly they grabbed one another's hands and hurried down the forest path. As the shadows deepened all around, they reached the lake. But now the littlest ones, Marta and Caroline, were too tired to go on.

"We'll rest a little here," said Nicholas, who was the oldest. "Then we'll run the rest of the way home."

"It's so far around the lake," complained Charlotte. "We'll never be home in time. Mother is going to get so mad."

"I wish we had a horse," said Molly. "How quickly we could get home then!"

No sooner had she spoken those words than along came a beautiful white horse. His coat shimmered in the twilight. His long mane and tail flowed like silk as he trotted right up to the astonished children. Whinnying softly, he lowered his neck as though he wanted them to climb onto his back.

The children couldn't believe their luck. Without a moment's hesitation, Nicholas, the leader, climbed onto the horse's back.

"Come on, everyone," he called to the others. "Get on quickly."

"There won't be room for all seven of us," objected Molly, but she climbed onto the horse all the same. Then followed Christopher. Amazingly, there was still plenty of space on the horse's back, so Charlotte climbed up, and then Netty.

Even with five children on the horse, there was as much room as before, because as each child climbed up, the horse's back grew longer and longer.

Caroline was next, and the last one was Marta. She was the smallest. She jumped up and the others tried to pull her, but no matter how hard she tried, she couldn't climb up. The horse even knelt down to try to help her, but she still couldn't get her short legs over the horse's back.

Frustrated, Marta called out to her big brother Nicholas to help. But Marta was so young that she still couldn't speak properly, so she called out, "Nikka, Nikka, help me up!"

In that instant, right from under the children, the white horse disappeared. All that was left of him was a ripple on the surface of the lake and something shimmering in the deep.

The children tumbled to the ground in a great big pile-up. But they didn't mind, for now they understood that it was a water horse whom they had met. He thought it was his own name, "Neckan," that Marta had called out, and he vanished when he heard it. It was little Marta, who could not even speak properly, who saved them all from vanishing under the water.

River Sprites

The river sprite lives behind waterfalls, where he plays his fiddle. Because he can change shape, there are different descriptions of him, though most say he is small and slender and very handsome. His skin is pale and he has long, wavy black hair.

Not every waterfall has a river sprite. But if you find one, you might be able to persuade him to teach you his music. Go on a Thursday and take a leg of mutton—he loves mutton. But don't be skimpy with the bone. If you give him one with almost no meat, he'll only teach you how to tune your instrument.

Many of the greatest fiddle players say they learned their art from the sprite. But you must be careful. The sprite will teach you great music. He'll even teach you the River Sprite's Reel. He'll teach you the first part, the second part, and the third part. But you must never ever play the fourth part. That belongs to him.

Playing the Fourth Part

There was once a fiddler who had been taught by a river sprite. Naturally he was always in high demand at dances and weddings, for nobody could play as well as he. Where he played, the dancing was livelier and the mood better. So when the squire of Eskdale decided to hold a Midsummer Night's celebration, he invited the fiddler to play.

As soon as the meal was over, the fiddler began a lively piece. All the young people jumped up and began to dance. The fiddler played familiar tunes and new tunes, some that were fast and some that were slow. Soon the dance floor filled with people, swinging happily in time to the music.

As the evening drew nigh and dusk fell, the fiddler played better and better. His music soared and spun. The dancers twisted and twirled. The fiddler became so absorbed in his work that before he knew it he began to play the River Sprite's Reel.

Everyone in the room rose and began to dance. The old danced and the young danced and everyone who could walk danced. The fiddler played harder and faster, faster and harder, till he grew so excited that he completely forgot himself—and he began to play the fourth part of the reel.

Now everything began to move, not just the young and the old, but the blind and the lame too. The babies rose out of their cradles and began to dance through the air. Next the tables and chairs, the cups and saucers, the ale mugs and wine goblets, rose into the air and spun around to the River Sprite's Reel. On and on played

Although not many people have seen a river sprite, many have heard the music he plays. It is so exquisitely beautiful that it can make you weep. The next time you visit a waterfall, listen carefully. Perhaps you will hear his fiddle.

the fiddler. He played till his fingers spurted blood, and still he couldn't stop, and everything and everyone kept on dancing.

At this time a dairymaid named Bridget was on her way to join the festivities. She was late because she had been milking the cows. On her way to the pasture that morning, she had found a four-leaf clover and this she had pinned to her bodice.

As she neared the farmhouse, she heard the wild music playing and wondered what was going on. It seemed to her that everything, even the trees, had begun to sway and move to the music coming from the great hall. She hurried to the house, and when she opened the door she was astonished. Inside, the old and the young spun madly around. The air was filled with swirling objects and nobody seemed able to stop. Bridget looked up at the fiddler to tell him to end the music, and then she saw him—the river sprite! He stood right behind the fiddler, and *he* was controlling the playing. She could plainly see him because of the four-leaf clover she had pinned to her bodice.

Quickly the dairymaid fished a knife out of her pocket, dashed up to the fiddler, and cut the strings on his fiddle. The moment she did, the sprite vanished, the music stopped, and everyone fell down, exhausted.

It was a lucky thing that Bridget cut the strings, for if she hadn't, the river sprite would have compelled them to dance themselves to death. That's the punishment he gives for playing the music that belongs to him.

One young boy was so desperate to learn to play the fiddle that he sat by the waterfall every night, hacking away at his instrument. In the end, the river sprite, who really likes peace and quiet, became so annoyed that he taught the boy to play just so he wouldn't have to listen to the terrible noise.

Selkies

Some hidden folk live in the ocean. The best known of these ocean dwellers are the mermaids and mermen. But there are other beings that many don't know because they look like ordinary seals. Called selkies, these people live in a marvelous kingdom at the bottom of the sea. Their houses are beautiful, decorated with pearls, seashells, and other treasures. Some even have gardens planted with lovely fronds of seaweed and surrounded by fences made of electric eels.

When the selkies are in their underwater world, they take human form and look just like us. But to travel or come up to the surface they must put on sealskin. Once on land, they can take off their skin and enjoy our world, but usually they do this only on Midsummer Night's Eve, the longest day of the year. Then they climb onto the sand or the smooth rocks along the seashore to dance and play in the twilight.

The Selkie Wife

One fine Midsummer Night's Eve, a fisherman from Shetland happened to be walking along a small bay. The soft rays from the setting sun sparkled on the water and played with the lengthening shadows. At the far end of the bay the fisherman saw shadows moving on the smooth rocks that jutted out into the sea. As he came closer, he saw that the shadows were actually beautiful people dancing. On the ground nearby lay several sealskins, and the man understood then that these people were the hidden folk called selkies.

Quietly, so as not to disturb them, the man drew nearer and crouched low beside a bush. But a twig snapped under his foot, and the selkies saw him. Terrified, they snatched up their skins, slipped them on, and plunged into the sea.

One maiden ran back and forth, crying out in a strange yet beautiful language. She kept approaching the bush where the fisherman stood, looking pleadingly at him. The fisherman looked around to see what she wanted, and then he saw her skin neatly tucked under the bush where he had been hiding. He picked it up, but when he looked into her lovely face and bewitching brown eyes, he could not give her the skin.

"Don't go back," he said. "Stay here with me and be my wife. Your friends and family will soon forget you. I will love and cherish you forever, and you shall want for nothing."

She shook her head wildly and pointed beseechingly to her skin. But the fisherman hardened his heart.

"You cannot return," he said, holding on to the skin firmly.

At length the seal maiden understood that the fisherman would never give back her sealskin, and she went with him to his home, where he locked her skin in a box.

They were married and settled down in his house near the sea. In time they had

several children, who were in every way like human beings except that they had thin webs between their fingers and toes.

The Shetlander truly loved his wife, and she came to love him too. But although she loved her children dearly and cared for her husband, she always longed for the sea. Often she walked down to the bay to sit on the flat rocks. Then a large male seal would swim up to the surface and the two would speak to each other in their strange, beautiful language.

She returned from these meetings thoughtful and sad. This made the fisherman uneasy, so he always made sure his wife's sealskin was securely locked up. He carried the key in his belt while he was away at sea.

Thus the years glided by, and the selkie woman's hopes of leaving the upper world nearly vanished. Then one day, when the children were outside playing, one of the boys happened to find a key.

"Look, Mother," he said proudly. "It's Father's key. It must have fallen off his belt."

The selkie woman's heart beat fast and hard.

"Here, my son. Give it to me," she said, trembling with excitement. She took the key and opened the box. There lay her sealskin. It was neatly folded and as soft and supple as the day she took it off. Carefully, she lifted it out and stroked it. Then she gathered her children around and, for the first time, told them of her life below the sea. They looked at her with wondering eyes as they learned of their other family down in the deep.

"I must return to my first family now," she said. "I will always love you and watch over you. If ever you need me, come to the rocks in the evening."

She kissed and hugged her children one last time. Then she grabbed her sealskin and ran off to the bay. Slipping easily into her skin, she leaped joyfully into the sea. At once, the large seal with whom she used to talk joined her.

When the fisherman learned what had happened, he ran in despair down to the rocks. He called for his wife, but to no avail. He never saw her again.

But whenever the children were sad or lonesome, they went down to the bay. Then a beautiful seal with large brown eyes would swim to them and speak in a soft, strange tongue that they gradually came to understand. And every Midsummer Night's Eve, the selkie woman's children gathered on the smooth rocks in the bay. Then their mother joyfully greeted them, and they laughed and played with their selkie brothers and sisters, grandparents, and cousins, aunts, and uncles the whole night long, and nobody ever tried to steal sealskins again.

Source Note

In contrast to traditional folktales, in which the emotional truth of a story is more important than its literal truth, these stories belong to a group of tales originally told as fact. As a consequence, they tend to be very brief and anecdotal in their original form, like whispered rumors of strange happenings. These are the stories my mother, aunt, and grandmother told me, almost in passing, so that I would know what the world is really like and what I could find if I paid close attention.

To make these tales engaging to today's children, I have had to flesh them out considerably, filling in the gaps left by tellers and audiences who shared a vast and intimate knowledge of these hidden folk and their ways. Always I have grounded my writing in traditional lore and legend.

References

Arrowsmith, Nancy, with George Moorse. *A Field Guide to the Little People*. London: Macmillan, 1977.

Briggs, Katharine. *Abbey Lubbers, Banshees, and Boggarts: An Illustrated Encyclopedia of Fairies*. New York: Pantheon Books, 1979.

————. *The Vanishing People: Fairy Lore and Legend*. New York: Pantheon Books, 1978.

Bø, Olav. *Norsk Folkediktning III: Segner (Norwegian Folklore III: Legends)*. Oslo, Norway: Det Norske Samlaget, 1977.

Craigie, William A. *Scandinavian Folk-Lore*. London: Alexander Gardner, 1896.

Keightley, Thomas. *The Fairy Mythology*. London: Methuen, 1892.

Kvideland, Reimund, and Henning K. Sehmsdorf, editors. *Scandinavian Folk Belief and Legend*. Minneapolis: University of Minnesota Press, 1988.

Leach, Maria, editor. *Funk and Wagnalls Standard Dictionary of Folklore, Mythology and Legend*. New York: Funk and Wagnalls, 1950.

McHargue, Georgess. *The Impossible People*. New York: Holt, Rinehart and Winston, 1972.

Rose, Carol. *Spirits, Fairies, Leprechauns, and Goblins: An Encyclopedia*. New York: W.W. Norton and Company, 1996.